D1198874

Folk Tales and Legends

North American Folklore

Folk Tales and Legends

by Ellyn Sanna

Mason Crest Publishers

Mason Crest Publishers Inc.
370 Reed Road
Broomall, Pennsylvania 19008
(866) MCP-BOOK (toll free)
www.masoncrest.com

First printing
1 2 3 4 5 6 7 8 9 10
Library of Congress Cataloging-in-Publication Data on file at the Library of Congress.
ISBN 1-59084-346-0
     1-59084-328-2 (series)

Design by Lori Holland.
Composition by Bytheway Publishing Services, Binghamton, New York.
Cover design by Joe Gilmore.
Printed and bound in the Hashemite Kingdom of Jordan.

Picture credits:
J. Rowe: pp. 6, 8, 17, 18, 20, 23, 30, 33, 37, 40, 45, 48, 50, 53, 54, 55, 56, 58, 60, 62, 64, 68, 70, 74, 78, 84, 86, 92, 97, 100
PhotoDisc: pp. 11, 14, 38, 66, 82, 90
Cover: "Land of Enchantment" by Norman Rockwell © 1923 SEPS: Licensed by Curtis Publishing, Indianapolis, IN. www.curtispublishing.com

Printed by permission of the Norman Rockwell Family
© the Norman Rockwell Family Entities

Contents

Folklore grows from long-ago
seeds. Just as an acorn sends
down roots even as it shoots up
leaves across the sky, folklore is
rooted deeply in the past and
yet still lives and grows today.
It spreads through our modern
world with branches as wide
and sturdy as any oak's;
it grounds us in yesterday even
as it helps us make sense of
both the present and the future.

INTRODUCTION

by Dr. Alan Jabbour

WHAT DO A TALE, a joke, a fiddle tune, a quilt, a jig, a game of jacks, a saint's day procession, a snake fence, and a Halloween costume have in common? Not much, at first glance, but all these forms of human creativity are part of a zone of our cultural life and experience that we sometimes call "folklore."

The word "folklore" means the cultural traditions that are learned and passed along by ordinary people as part of the fabric of their lives and culture. Folklore may be passed along in verbal form, like the urban legend that we hear about from friends who assure us that it really happened to a friend of their cousin. Or it may be tunes or dance steps we pick up on the block, or ways of shaping things to use or admire out of materials readily available to us, like that quilt our aunt made. Often we acquire folklore without even fully realizing where or how we learned it.

Though we might imagine that the word "folklore" refers to cultural traditions from far away or long ago, we actually use and enjoy folklore as part of our own daily lives. It is often ordinary, yet we often remember and prize it because it seems somehow very special. Folklore is culture we share with others in our communities, and we build our identities through the sharing. Our first shared identity is family identity, and family folklore such as shared meals or prayers or songs helps us develop a sense of belonging. But as we grow older we learn to belong to other groups as well. Our identities may be ethnic, religious, occupational, or regional—or all of these, since no one has only one cultural identity. But in every case, the identity is anchored and strengthened by a variety of cultural traditions in which we participate and share with our neighbors. We feel the threads of connection with people we know, but the threads extend far beyond our own immediate communities. In a real sense, they connect us in one way or another to the world.

Folklore possesses features by which we distinguish ourselves from each other. A certain dance step may be African American, or a certain story urban, or a certain hymn Protestant, or a certain food preparation Cajun. Folklore can distinguish us, but at the same time it is one of the best ways we introduce ourselves to each other. We learn about new ethnic groups on the North American landscape by sampling their cuisine, and we enthusiastically adopt musical ideas from other communities. Stories, songs, and visual designs move from group to group, enriching all people in the process. Folklore thus is both a sign of identity, experienced as a special marker of our special groups, and at the same time a cultural coin that is well spent by sharing with others beyond our group boundaries.

Folklore is usually learned informally. Somebody, somewhere, taught us that jump rope rhyme we know, but we may have trouble remembering just where we got it, and it probably wasn't in a book that was assigned as homework. Our world has a domain of formal knowledge, but folklore is a domain of knowledge and culture that is learned by sharing and imitation rather than formal instruction. We can study it formally—that's what we are doing now!—but its natural arena is in the informal, person-to-person fabric of our lives.

Not all culture is folklore. Classical music, art sculpture, or great novels are forms of high art that may contain folklore but are not themselves folklore. Popular music or art may be built on folklore themes and traditions, but it addresses a much wider and more diverse audience than folk music or folk art. But even in the world of popular and mass culture, folklore keeps popping up around the margins. E-mail is not folklore—but an e-mail smile is. And college football is not folklore—but the wave we do at the stadium is.

This series of volumes explores the many faces of folklore throughout the North American continent. By illuminating the many aspects of folklore in our lives, we hope to help readers of the series to appreciate more fully the richness of the cultural fabric they either possess already or can easily encounter as they interact with their North American neighbors.

A tale from Africa explains the beginning of stories.

ONE

Stories and Storytellers
Power and Magic

It was a dark and stormy night. . . .

*I*T WAS A DARK *and stormy night. Three men sat around the campfire. One said, "John, tell us a story." So John began:*

"It was a dark and stormy night. Three men sat around the campfire. One said, 'John, tell us a story.' So John began:

"'It was a dark and stormy night. Three men sat around the campfire. One said, "John, tell us a story." So John began. . . .

If you've ever camped out or slept overnight at a pajama party, chances are you heard this endless story. Nothing ever happens; we're trapped in the loop of John's story, like a mirror reflecting a mirror, endlessly into eternity. And yet there's still something gripping and mysterious about that dark, stormy night; something about those three men huddled around their campfire fascinates us. The words are more than just a word game; they have power.

All stories have power. And in the centuries before televisions, radios, and CD players, human beings' amusement often depended on their own voices. The word "tale" comes from an Anglo-Saxon word that means "speech"—and folktales were meant to be told out loud. Like John and his two friends, people spoke their stories around the fire at night, whiling away the long dark hours until daylight.

At first these stories may have been merely a way of spreading news, the way today we watch the evening news on television or pick up a newspaper. "Did you hear about what happened over the mountain?" the story may have begun, and what followed would have been a factual account of recent events.

But some of these accounts were so exciting that they were repeated over and over down through the years, until the new generation learned the stories and retold them to their own children. As the years went by, these stories changed and grew. New details were added, while some were forgotten. They were no longer strictly factual accounts (although people probably still regarded them as "true").

Those who could tell the best tales, who knew the most stories and could hold their audiences enthralled, came to hold a special place in the community. These people were valuable (more valuable than the most expensive big-screen TV!), and they possessed a

THE STORY BEHIND WORDS

Another root word for "tale" has to do with counting. That's where the word "teller" comes from; you might think a teller is one who tells a tale, but in today's usage, a teller usually works at a bank and counts money. But we might also say that we "recount a story"—and in this case, we don't mean we counted the story over again, but that we told a story. The reason for the closeness between counting and telling has to do with the fact that the earliest stories were often rhymed; storytellers spoke with a rhythm, counting off the beats of the words.

Talking inanimate objects and animals are common in folktales.

power that seemed nearly magical to the others in their communities. With their words they were able to recreate the past; with the strength of their speech they could make new worlds; and by the magic of their voice they could bring wisdom and insight to their listeners.

Stories brought people knowledge, comfort, and inspiration. No matter what their present circumstances, through the power of a story, people in strange lands could go home again . . . find courage for current hardships . . . take hope in the assurance of a divine or supernatural order that governed the world. When people from Africa came to North America as slaves, for instance, they had lost nearly everything—but no one could steal their stories.

Some say these stories came from the gods themselves. . . .

ANANSI, the spider, wanted the sky god's stories. But the sky god would not give them to Anansi. "Huh!" the sky god laughed. "Stories must be bought—and what makes you think you could afford them?"

Anansi and Br'er Rabbit are not the only tricksters that show up in North American folktales. Coyote was a trickster character in Native American tales from the Southwest, and the Yankee Peddler was a Northeastern trickster. Greek Americans tell about the trickster Nastradin Hodja.

Many cultures have **venerated** storytellers.

- Ivan the Terrible is said to have been unable to sleep unless three old blind men told him folktales.
- In some African tribes, the storyteller was one of the most important members in the society; his job was to chant **genealogies**, advise the ruler, and keep track of the tribe's history.
- In ancient Ireland, except for during times of war, the storyteller was second only to the king. The storyteller studied his art for 15 years, and he had to know 250 primary tales and a hundred less important ones.
- In Siberia, lumbermen, fishermen, and hunters hired skilled storytellers to help them pass their leisure time.
- Hungarian soldiers, according to a centuries-old custom, can be asked to tell bedtime stories to their comrades—or pay the penalty of shouting into the stove: "Oh Mother, haven't you brought me up to be a big brute who hasn't even been taught to tell a tale!"
- Navajo storytellers were important to their people's religion. They recited long creation stories that last two to three days.

"What is the price of the stories?" Anansi asked.

"They can be bought for nothing less than a black snake, a wild dog, a black cat, a swarm of hornets, and a fairy.

The spider smiled. "I will bring all of these things. What's more, I will throw in my own mother."

The sky god laughed once more. "I will believe you when I see what you have brought."

Anansi went to his old mother and asked her advice. She was

The wonder and magic of folktales appeals to children.

Immigrants from Japan brought with them this endless story:

Long ago all the rats in Nagasaki got together and decided that since there was nothing left to eat on their island, they would cross to Satsuma. So they boarded a ship and set out—but on their way, they met a boatload of rats coming from the other direction. As luck would have it, there was nothing to eat in Satsuma either. So the rats decided to jump into the sea and drown.

The first rat began to cry, "Chu chu!" and jumped overboard with a splash. Then another rat cried, "Chu chu!" and jumped overboard with a splash. Then another rat cried, "Chu chu!" and jumped overboard with a splash. Then another rat. . .

even more crafty than her son, and she whispered in his ear what he should do. With her tricks, Anansi was able to trap the black snake, the wild dog, the black cat, and the swarm of hornets. One by one, he brought them to the sky god.

"Hmph!" the sky god said. "I still don't see a fairy."

Anansi went back to his home and carved a baby out of wood. Then he plastered the doll with sticky sap, and placed it at the foot of a tree, where fairies often came to play. He put in a mess of pounded yams in the baby's wooden hands, and finally, he tied a string around the baby's neck and hid himself behind a tree to watch and wait.

Before long, a fairy flew down and looked at the wooden baby. "May I eat some of your yam mash?" she asked the doll.

Anansi pulled on the string to make the doll's head nod.

The fairy called to her sister, "She says I may eat her yams."

"So eat them then," the sister answered.

The fairy ate the mashed yam and smiled at the baby. "Thank you!"

African Americans kept the heritage of their ancestors alive by telling the stories of Africa generation after generation. In North America, however, the stories gradually changed, as the people adapted to the new realities of their lives. Anansi the spider was sometimes called Aunt Nancy—and sometimes he merged with Br'er Rabbit, a trickster who used a sticky tar baby to get what he wanted.

The doll of course said nothing. The fairy frowned. "I told her thank you," she called to her sister, "but she doesn't answer me."

"So slap her," the sister shouted.

Pow! The fairy slapped the wooden doll—and the fairy's hand stuck fast to the sticky sap. "She won't let me go!" the fairy cried to her sister.

"So slap her again with your other hand," came her sister's advice.

Pow! Now the fairy's other hand was stuck. "She has both my hands now, and she won't let go," the fairy whined.

"So kick her with your feet," her sister replied.

Bam! Bim! The fairy kicked the doll with her feet—and now she was stuck on both ends to the wooden baby. Anansi came out from behind the tree laughing.

"You fool! Now I have you."

He tied her up and slung her over his back. Then he went to his mother. "Come along," he told the old spider woman and lifted her off her feet.

"Sky god," he shouted, "here I have the fairy you wanted—and my old mother I promised you as well."

The sky god looked at Anansi the spider and nodded. "Great kings could not buy my stories, but you have kept your promise. Today I take my stories and I give them all to you with my blessing. No more shall they be called sky god stories. Now they are spider stories.

A Mexican American folktale explains why humans live as long as they do.

TWO

Myths and Legends
Why the World Is the Way It Is

Curiosity can be a serious flaw, as this folktale demonstrates.

THE BLACKFOOT TRIBE tells this story about how the stars came to have their places in the sky. Like the biblical story of Adam and Eve, this story also contains a warning about the importance of obedience. Parents used stories like these both to explain the world to their children and to instruct them in the way they should behave.

Two young women of the tribe loved to take their beds away from where the others were camped and lie looking up at the stars as they fell asleep. As they watched the stars night after night, one of them noticed that a particular star was more beautiful than all the rest.

"See that white star?" she asked her friend. "That is my favorite. I wish it could be my husband. If I were to marry that star, I would live in the sky."

The next day, while she was picking berries alone, the young woman heard a small noise behind her. She turned and found a young man, dressed all in white leather, with white feathers in his hair.

"Do not be afraid." He smiled. "I am the white star you wished to marry. I have come for you. Marry me and live with me among the stars."

The girl did not hesitate. She gave her hand to the young man, and they began their journey to the sky. There the Star Husband took her to meet his father the Sun and his mother the Moon. Moon liked her new daughter-in-law and set about teaching her what she would need to know to live in the star world.

WHY THE WHITES HAVE EVERYTHING

When African Americans looked at North American society, a society that claimed to be founded on equality and justice, they couldn't help but wonder about their own situation. They created myths to explain the world they knew, where God was blamed for the inequalities the African American faced.

According to one such story, when God was making the world, he called all the people to come and get into one of two bags. The white people got into a big heavy bag that was already full of things—money, land, all sorts of riches. But the black people got into a little light bag that didn't have anything at all in it. And that's why white folk got it all and black folk didn't.

In Daryl Cumber Dance's book, *Shuckin' and Jivin'*, he asserts that these myths do not reflect African Americans' acceptance of their situation as God's will for them. Instead, they are not true myths, but actually jokes—and the butt of these jokes is racism.

"Here is a magic digging stick," she told the young woman. "You may use this to find roots that are good to eat. Take as many roots as you want, but be careful—there is one root you must never take." The Moon took the young woman to a brushy place where the thorns and thickets grew around a single thick green stem. "See that turnip plant?" the Moon said to her daughter-in-law. "You must never pull it from where it grows. Do you understand?"

The girl nodded. She had no intention of ever pulling the turnip from its place. Living with her Star Husband, she had everything she needed; she had no interest in a turnip.

As the months passed, she was always very careful to dig around the turnip plant and never touch it. She and her Star Husband were happy together, and their joy increased when she gave birth to a baby boy.

But as their child grew, the young woman's thoughts began to wander. She found herself obsessed with the turnip plant, and she sat for hours at a time staring at it. "I wonder why I cannot pull that plant," she mused. "Maybe Moon is being selfish and wants to keep it all to herself."

The more she brooded about the plant, the more she could not stop thinking about it. What kind of turnip was it, that it should be so important? Did it possess some magic power?

One day, the woman yielded to temptation. She grabbed the turnip and tugged it out of the ground. Whish! A burst of air rose up from the hole where the turnip had grown. The woman peeked down through the hole; far, far below, she saw the Earth. She could even see the lodges of her own people.

When her husband found out what she had done, he turned pale. "Now that you have looked upon the Earth, you can no longer stay here in the sky. You must return to your people with our son. But be very careful. Do not let our son touch the earth for 14 days. If he does, he will turn into a star, one that never moves but always stays in one place."

With many tears, the Star Husband, the Sun, and the Moon said good-bye to the woman and her son. Then the Sun Father

made a rope of spider webs and carefully lowered the woman and her baby down through the turnip hole to the Earth below.

Her people greeted her with joy, and the young woman told them all about the sky world where she had lived with her Star Husband. She warned them that they must help her keep her son from touching the Earth for 14 days.

For 13 days things went well, and the young woman settled back into her old life. On the 14th day, her mother asked her to get some water from the river. The young woman hesitated, but her son was asleep on his bed of furs. "If he wakes," she warned her mother, "do not let him crawl onto the Earth."

The grandmother laughed to herself after her daughter left; she could see no reason why her grandson could not touch the Earth, and so when he woke from his nap, she let him crawl about his blankets. One little hand touched the Earth. "There, you see," she said, "nothing—"

But her voice trailed into silence, for her grandson had disappeared.

That night, the young woman went back to the place where she had once wished for a husband. She watched the stars come out one by one. High in the top of the sky, where she had pulled the turnip, she saw a new star. She knew it was her son.

And the star-that-does-not-move is still there.

> An old German story is very similar to the Southwestern folktale about why humans live as long as they do. In the German version, the man also gets the monkey's years at the end of his life. Variations of stories appear around the world.

The stories of Hispanic Americans in the Southwest are a mixture of native legends and folklore from Spain. This humorous story explains why human beings age the way they do.

When God created the world, he decided to give humans two friends: the burro and the dog. Then he called the three friends to stand in front of him and told the human being, "You are a human being, and you will live 60 years. During your lifetime you will see good days and hard days, but there will be more good days than bad."

The human being thought that 60 years was too short a lifespan, but he nodded his head.

Then God turned to the burro. "You are a burro, and you will serve the human being. You will live 30 years, and during your lifetime you will see good days and hard days, but there will be more hard days than good."

The burro sighed. "If my life is to be so hard, I don't want to live so many years. Take away ten of those 30 years you promised me."

The human being stepped forward. "Lord, if it's no trouble, give those ten years he doesn't want to me."

So God added the ten years to the human being's 60. Then he spoke to the dog. "You are a dog, and you will be a good friend to the human being, but you will have to obey him. You will live 20 years, and during your lifetime you will have good days and bad, but there will be more bad days than good."

The dog gave a mournful howl. "If that's the case, I don't want to live so many years. Take away at least five years."

CULTURAL VIEWPOINTS ON OLD AGE

The lives of many Hispanic Americans were hard; the ability to labor and produce concrete and tangible products was often valued. Other cultures, however, valued old age for its more intangible gifts—for instance, wisdom.

According to an old Celtic tale from the British Isles, nine hazel trees grew around a sacred pool, dropping their nuts into the water. The Celts valued all trees, believing that each tree had its own gifts to offer; according to their beliefs, the hazel gave wisdom. An old salmon swimming in the sacred pool ate the nuts and became the wisest creature in the land. The longer he lived, the more he ate, and the wiser he became. (The number of bright spots on salmon were said to indicate how many nuts they had eaten.)

According to the Irish version of this tale, a wise teacher caught the salmon. He told his pupil to cook the fish but not eat any of it. However, as the fish fried, hot juice spattered onto the apprentice's thumb, which he stuck into his mouth to cool. The pupil was called Fionn Mac Cumhail, and he went on to become one of the most heroic leaders in Irish mythology. Thanks to the ancient salmon, Fionn Mac Cumhail became wise without having to live long years.

The human being stepped forward again. "Lord, I'll take the years he doesn't want."

So God gave the human being the years the dog didn't want. And that is why human beings live the life of a donkey from 60 to 70—and why they live like dogs from their 70th year on!

In North America, the African spider Anansi was transformed into Aunt Nancy—and Br'er Rabbit.

THREE

Wisdom Tales
Sharing Knowledge and Insight

Anansi tried to collect all the wisdom in the world in his pumpkin.

THE WORD "WISDOM" comes from Old English words that had to do with knowing. Wisdom is different than mere factual knowledge, though. Instead, it has to do with insight into how things work at the deepest levels. According to some traditions, wisdom is even seen as the embodiment of God's will at work in the world.

Cultures from all over the world have valued wisdom. They have told stories about wisdom—and they have told stories as a way to pass wisdom along. Early African Americans told this story to explain how wisdom came to humanity in the first place.

Anansi the spider thought that if he could collect all the wisdom in the world, he would have power over everyone. Everyone would have to come to him for the answers to their problems—and he could charge them plenty of money for the solutions he gave them.

So Anansi went around the world collecting all the wisdom he could find, stuffing it into a big pumpkin. When at last the pumpkin was full and he couldn't find any more wisdom anywhere in the world, he decided to hide the pumpkin at the top of a tall tree where no one would find it.

Anansi tied the pumpkin around his neck with a piece of rope, so that the pumpkin rested on his belly, and then he started climbing the tree. He couldn't go very fast, though, because the big pumpkin kept getting in his way.

A little boy stood at the foot of the tree watching Anansi. Finally the boy burst out laughing. "Silly spider," he said, "why don't you put the pumpkin on your back so you can climb better?"

Anansi froze. The boy was right, he knew—and that meant the little boy had a piece of wisdom that somehow Anansi had missed. Anansi was so angry and frustrated that he grabbed the pumpkin from around his neck and threw it on the ground.

The pumpkin burst open, and the wisdom inside it scattered in a million pieces. The breeze blew the pieces of wisdom over the world. Everyone got a little bit—but no one got it all.

Another African American tale offers wise advice against envying other's situations.

Poor old Moses was bowed down with troubles. In fact, his trouble were so big and so heavy, he could hardly do his work. But one dark night, he heard the devil calling, "Come here, everybody. Come and listen!" So Moses stumbled over to see what the devil had to say.

"I'm tired of hearing you all complain about your troubles," the devil told the crowd that had gathered around him. "You're so busy thinking about your troubles, you don't have time for sinning. So I want you all to give me your troubles. That's right, folks. Wrap those troubles up and hand them over. Then you can go back to old-fashioned sinning."

Moses could hardly believe his ears. He hurried home and began packing up his troubles in the biggest crate he could fine. First, he put in his rheumatism, and then he stuffed in the debts he owed his landlord and the storekeeper. Next, he dropped in the tooth that had been hurting him and the broken plow that

Old Moses realized the wisdom of accepting his own troubles.

Arab Americans tell this story of tragic wisdom:

A man was hunting with his son, when a ghoul attacked them and killed the boy. Weighed down with sorrow for his son, the man returned home with the deer he had killed. He hid his grief from his wife and said, "Take this meat I have caught and cook it—but I will eat it only if it has been cooked in a pot that was never used for a meal of sorrow."

The woman went to her neighbors, seeking such a pot. One neighbor shook her head and said, "We used the big pot for the rice the night my husband died." Another sighed and said, "We boiled our vegetables in our pot the day the baby took sick and died." One by one, they each told her a story of yet another sorrowful meal. She returned to her husband empty-handed.

"No household has escaped sorrow," she told him. "There is no pot that has not cooked a meal of mourning."

"And it is our turn now," the man told his wife. Tears filled his eyes as he told her of their son's death.

The storyteller concludes with these words: "Of such things and the like is the world made, but fortunate is the soul that God loves and calls to himself."

wouldn't keep a straight line. He crammed in his own son, who'd been acting mighty rebellious lately—and then he slipped his wife's nagging tongue in along the side of the crate. Last of all, he shed his own black skin, folded it up, and slapped it on the top of all the rest of his troubles.

Moses tied the crate with a piece of rope, and then he set off to give it to the devil. He found the street outside his house packed with people, all eager to get rid of their troubles. To his amazement, Sister Thompson, who was always laughing as though she didn't have a care in the world, was there with an enormous bag on her shoulders. Even the preacher had a big pack on his back.

One of the devil's helpers stepped up to Moses and stamped his crate of troubles, then handed him a receipt.

"I don't want no receipt," Moses cried. "I'm not planning on ever taking that crate back, no way, no how."

"That's not your receipt," the helper explained. "It's someone else's. The devil had such a big response to his offer, that he's decided he can't keep all these troubles. Instead, he's just going to shift everything around a bit. Come Tuesday, you have to come back with this receipt, and then you'll pick up someone else's load of troubles—and some-one else will have yours. Every-one says that their troubles are worse than anyone else's, so this way, everyone should be happy."

Moses scratched his chin. He might get a pack of troubles that held only a bit of dandruff, he rea-soned. Or he might end up with a wife that was too pretty for her own good, or more money than

he'd know how to handle. That thought made him grin, and he headed on back home.

But the more he thought about it, the more he worried. The devil wasn't known for helping people out much, he realized. So when Tuesday came, Moses went up to the devil and said, "I've changed my mind, sir. I've grown kind of attached to those troubles I had, and I'd like them back after all."

The devil just twitched his tail and laughed. "Moses, let me see your receipt."

So Moses showed him the receipt, and the devil gave a twisty smile that looked like someone had taken a knife to his face. "Why, Moses, you got lucky. Let me congratulate you. You have just a little bundle of white-folk troubles coming your way. What a relief that will be to you." The devil reached down and held up a small burlap sack. "See? This is yours now."

Moses leaned forward and peeked inside the sack. Then he pulled his head back with a gasp. "Please," he said, "I'd like my own troubles back."

He fussed so long and so loud that at last the devil got mad. "All right, all right!" The devil reached into the pile of troubles and tossed Moses' old crate at him. "Take them and leave. But don't let me ever hear you fussing about your troubles again."

Moses threw his crate up on his shoulder as though it were filled with feathers. When he got home, his wife couldn't believe her eyes.

"Why did you go and bring all that old stuff back?" she asked him.

Moses explained what had happened, but his wife just stamped her foot. "Moses, you fool, you could have had some white man's tiny little troubles instead of that big crate full of heartache."

Moses let out a long sigh of contentment. "No, ma'am. I didn't want that white man's troubles—'cause when I looked inside that burlap sack, I saw a little old stomach cancer snuggled right up to a coffin."

In many of the Jack tales, the hero encounters a giant.

FOUR

Heroes
Tales of the Best of Us

Jack's foolishness brought him good fortune.

EVER SINCE STORIES have been told, people have been inspired by tales of heroes, men and women who were stronger, braver, brighter than the rest of us. People like this give us all courage, and their stories fill us with wonder and hope.

These hero stories often follow traditional patterns. For instance, heroes often rise from places where you would least expect to find them. Many times they are the youngest daughter, the poorest son, the child who appears most foolish and least promising. They often must go on some sort of quest, seeking a magic object that will give them great power, and on their journey they encounter various trials and tests that must be overcome. The number three is often significant (at least in European stories; American Indians like stories with fours), and they sometimes must descend into another world before they can achieve their goal.

Some of the oldest hero tales in the English language are about a boy named Jack. Jack appears in story after story: sometimes he is the youngest of three brothers and he achieves good fortune through his kindness; sometimes he is the abused child of a cruel stepmother but is granted three wishes by an old beggar; and other times, he is the brave destroyer of a giant that threatens his homeland. By the 19th century, Jack had climbed the beanstalk to kill his giant, and his stories were among the most popular children's tales throughout England.

Jack also came to the New World, where he continued to

LARGER THAN LIFE HEROES

Many North American heroes possess amazing (and impossible) strength and cunning. Some examples of these tall-tale heroes are Paul Bunyan, the gigantic lumberman, and Pecos Bill, the cowboy.

have an assortment of adventures, especially in the Appalachian region of America. In 1943, Richard Chase collected these stories into *The Jack Tales*, making them famous. Jack had become a North American tradition.

Where the English Jack had depended on virtue and magic to save him, however, the North American Jack relied only on his own **ingenuity**. When he did encounter help, it came not from good witches and kindly gnomes, but from wealthy men who lent Jack money. North Americans apparently had a greater faith in humanity's ability to control its own destiny—and they pinned their hopes for a better future on wealth rather than the supernatural world.

The people in the Appalachian Mountains of the eastern United States tell this Jack story.

Once upon a time there was lazy boy named Jack who lived with his poor old mother. His mother did whatever she could to earn a living, a bit of sewing, a little spinning, a speck of baking now and then, but Jack would do nothing at all but bask in the summer sun and snooze by the hearth in the winter. At her wit's end, his mother finally told him that she could no longer feed him if he did not do what he could to help her make a living.

So Jack took himself off to the neighboring farm, where he worked for a day cleaning the barns. The farmer paid him a dime, but as Jack was coming home, he lost the dime in the creek.

"You stupid boy," his mother cried. "Why didn't you put the money in your pocket?"

Jack shrugged. "I'll do so another time."

The next day, he went back and did another day's work at the neighboring farm—and this time, the farmer paid him a jar of milk. Jack took the jar and carefully put into his pocket, just as his mother had told him to do, and headed home. Along the way, all the milk spilled out of the jar.

His mother was furious. "You foolish boy," she shouted, "you should have carried it in your hands."

Jack sighed. "I'll do so another time."

The next day, he went back to the farmer for another day's work. At the end of the day, the farmer gave Jack a pig. Jack re-

membered what his mother had told him, so he held the pig in his hands as he headed home—but the pig kicked and struggled so much that Jack finally dropped it. It ran off into the woods squealing, and Jack arrived home empty-handed yet again.

"Oh you silly boy," his mother said, too discouraged now to be angry. "Why couldn't you have carried the pig on your shoulder?"

"I'll do so another time," Jack said.

Some North American heroes were known not for their goodness but their astounding badness. Here are a few of those ne'er-do-wells:

- Belle Starr, the Bandit Queen
- Jesse James, the legendary bank robber
- Wild Bill Hickok, the gunslinger
- Stackalee, the African American outlaw

The next day, he worked for the farmer once again. At the end of the day, the farmer gave him a donkey. Jack had some trouble heaving the donkey onto his shoulder, but at last he got the donkey on his back and staggered off toward home.

As he stumbled along with the donkey braying on his back, he happened to pass the home of a rich man. This rich man

Many North American heroes were actual historical figures who grew to larger-than-life proportions. Here are some examples:

- Annie Oakley, the sharpshooter
- Davy Crockett, the backwoods politician
- Mike Fink, the Mississippi boatman
- Casey Jones, the railroad engineer
- Johnny Appleseed, who planted apples across North America
- George Washington, the leader who could not tell a lie

Annie Oakley was a real-life person who became a folk hero.

had a beautiful daughter who could not speak; the doctors said she would never recover unless she laughed, but the girl was so sad that she never even smiled. Her father had promised that he would give his daughter in marriage to the first man who could make her laugh.

When the girl looked out her window and saw Jack trudging along with the donkey kicking on his back, she gave a little sniff. Then her lips twitched. And finally, Jack and the donkey looked so silly that she burst out giggling. Immediately, she could speak again and called to her father to come see Jack.

JACK THE HERO

Jack is the most common name in folk tales and rhymes. Remember Jack Horner who sat in a corner? And then there was the Jack who jumped over the candlestick . . . and the Jack who went up the hill with his sister Jill . . . and Jack Sprat who was married to woman who only ate fat.

In countless folktales, Jack had adventures with giants and ogres, witches and beautiful princesses. He was always the younger, smaller fellow, the underdog with whom we all seem to identify—and in the end, he always got the treasure, killed the monster, married the princess . . . and lived happily ever after of course.

In some Appalachian Jack tales, Jack has two older
brothers named Will and Tom.

Her father was overjoyed. He kept his promise, and so Jack
married the rich man's daughter. Jack was now a wealthy man
himself. He and his wife and his old mother lived in a fine house
with everything they wanted for the rest of their lives.

How much does the moon weigh?

FIVE

Fools
Stories of Noodleheads and Numbskulls

Foolish John was one of those exasperating people who took everything literally.

THE JACK WHO shows up so often in North American folktales apparently had a cousin—Foolish John. In French-speaking regions, he is called Jean Sotte. Some of his adventures are very similar to Jack's, but unlike Jack who always triumphs, Foolish John always loses. The **Cajuns** of Louisiana tell this story about poor Foolish John.

One day, Foolish John put on his best clean clothes and set off for town. His mother sighed when she saw what he was wearing, for the sky was gray—and she hated to think how he would look when he returned.

"Foolish John," she called after him, "be careful not to get caught in the rain in your good clothes. If it starts to rain, be sure to duck out of it somewhere."

"All right, Mother," Foolish John said over his shoulder and continued on his way.

Just as he was crossing the bridge across the *bayou*, big raindrops began to fall on his head. He remembered what his mother had told him, but as he stood on the bridge, he could see nowhere to duck out of the rain. He thought and pondered and scratched his head.

Finally, he knew what he could do. He jumped off the bridge into the bayou and ducked his head down under the water. Now, he thought with satisfaction, the rain would not fall on his good clothes. His mother would be so pleased.

But when he returned home, his mother gasped at the sight of him, for he was covered with mud from head to toe. "Oh, Foolish John! Didn't I tell you to get out of the rain?"

51

"But I did," Foolish John answered. "I did exactly what you told me."

Pat and Mike are two Irishmen who show up in a number of folk-tales across northeastern Canada. Although Pat is a bit of a fool, sometimes, with his brother's help, he manages to outwit those in authority, as they do in this story from Nova Scotia.

An Irishman was out of work, so he went up to a government official and said, "Look, I've been voting for you all my life, and now you ought to do something for me. I want a job."

The man looked at him and said, "Well, now, Pat, I'll give you a job if you can answer three questions."

"Go ahead."

"Tell me, Pat," the government man said, "how much does the moon weigh?"

"That's easy," the Irishman said, "one hundred weight."

"How do you make that?" the official asked.

"Well," said the Irishman, "the moon has four quarters—and four quarters make a hundred."

The government man just shook his head. "Let me ask you my second question, Pat, and we'll see how you do. How many stars are in the sky?"

"Seven billion, eight thousand million, four hundred, and 52 thousand," the Irishman said promptly.

"How do you figure that?" asked the official.

The Irishman just shrugged. "If you don't believe me, go count them yourself. What's your next question?"

Some fool tales poke fun at outsiders to a region. For instance, people from the South tell the story of three travelers who were amazed by the size of Southern mosquitoes. Desperate to get away from the whining insects, the strangers hid in a shack in the midst of a swamp. In the night, they woke up to find blinking lights buzzing around the room.

"Let's get out of here," they shouted. "Those killer mosquitoes are back—and this time they've brought lanterns."

They ran all the way to the train station, where they took the first train home, never knowing they had run from harmless fireflies.

"This one is the hardest of all," the government man said with a crafty smile. "What am I thinking right now, Pat?"

The Irishman laughed. "You think I'm Pat—but I'm his brother Mike!"

Hispanic Americans in the Southwest tell this story of foolishness:

Five travelers were so tired that they slumped down beside the road. They were hungry and thirsty, but they were too tired to move. In fact, they were so tired that they could no longer even tell whose feet belonged to who.

Whose feet are whose?

A man passed by and saw them sitting there in a heap. "What are you doing there?" he asked them.

"We can't get up," they told him.

"Why not?"

"Because we're so tired we can't tell whose feet belongs to who."

"You fools!" the man laughed. "How much will you give me if I tell you whose feet are whose?"

They agreed on a price, and then the man took out a big stout needle. He stuck one of them in the foot.

"Ouch!"

"That's your foot," the man said. "Get up."

He stuck another one in the foot.

"Ouch!"

"That's yours," the man said.

One by one, he stuck them all with the needle, until they were all on their feet.

The ghost of the pirate LaFitte is rumored to haunt the bayous of Louisiana.

SIX

Ghosts and Horrors
Creepy Tales to Make
You Shudder

In folktales, ghosts often bring about justice.

WE ALL LOVE to shiver around a campfire as we listen to a good ghost story. This one, told in Virginia, has many variations told across the continent.

Once there was a tumbledown old house that had been haunted for years. People would dare each other to spend the night there, but no one was able to make it through until dawn. They were all too terrified by the ghost that drifted through the dark rooms.

Finally, a preacher took his Bible and went to the house. He built himself a fire, lit a lamp, and sat down to read. Before long, he thought he heard something way down in the cellar, like footsteps walking back and forth, back and forth. The preacher turned back to his Bible—but now he heard thump, thump, thump coming up the cellar stairs. After a few minutes, the door of the room where he was sitting creaked open.

The preacher jumped to his feet. "What do you want?" he hollered.

The door went gently shut. The preacher was trembling a little, but he sat down and began to read again. After a few moments, he again heard the step, step, step outside the door. This time the preacher held the Bible out in front of him and waited for the door to open.

Sure enough, the door creaked open. This time a young woman stood swaying in the doorway. Her skin was so tattered that he could see the white bones showing, and her hair was tangled and long. A blue light shone from the holes where her eyes should have been, and she had no nose at all.

"What do you want?" the preacher asked. His voice quavered, but he held tight to his Bible.

When the ghost spoke, her voice sounded like the wind blowing through the trees, coming and going, moaning and whispering. She told the preacher that her lover had killed her for her money and buried her in the cellar. If the preacher would dig up her bones and bury her properly, she would be able to rest at last.

The preacher found her bones, just as she had said, and he dug a hole and buried them in the graveyard. The ghost thanked him for his kindness—and then she handed him the end joint of her little finger from her left hand. "Lay this in the collection plate on Sunday," she told him, "and you will find out who murdered me."

She heaved a long tired sigh and sank into her grave as sweetly as though she were going to bed for a good night's sleep.

The next Sunday, the preacher did as the ghost had told him and laid the finger bone in the collection plate. One of the wealthiest men in the community dropped his offering into the plate, never noticing what lay there, but when his fingers brushed the bone, it stuck to his hand. He jumped to

his feet, rubbing and scrubbing at his hand, but he couldn't get the thing off him. Screaming, he confessed the murder, and the police took him to jail.

Some time later, the preacher went back to the house to be

One of the most famous North American ghost stories is the ghostly hitchhiker, a beautiful young girl who turns out to have died years ago. Variations of the story are told in all regions and all subcultures across the continent.

sure the ghost was still resting easy. He heard her voice whispering in the chimney, "Look under the hearth. My lover didn't get it all."

The preacher pried up the hearth—and there, sure enough, was a sack of money. He gave it to the poor, and the ghost was never heard from again.

In Louisiana, the ghost of the pirate Jean Lafitte is said to haunt the bayous where he buried his treasure before he died.

A young man was making his way back home after being away at war when a sudden storm drove him into an abandoned house for shelter. He built a fire, and with the rain beating on the roof, the young man settled down to sleep.

In the middle of the night, he shivered and woke up, convinced that he was no longer alone in the house. "Who's there?" he whispered.

By the light of the dying fire, he saw a shadowy figure stand-

The living tradition and active faith of nearly all countries abound in ghost legends. Not only may thousands of people be found who testify to having seen ghosts, but practices are all but universal which assume for their justification a substratum of such belief.

—*Stith Thompson*

ing with folded arms, a pirate's **cutlass** hanging at his side. "Come with me," the ghostly figure said.

"Who—who are you?" the young man asked.

"I am Jean Lafitte," the ghost wailed. "Come save my soul. Help me!" And with that he disappeared in the darkness.

The young man's heart was thudding, but he told himself he must have been dreaming and settled down to sleep again. He had just drifted off, when again he heard the wailing voice.

"Save my soul. Help me!"

"What do you want from me?" the young man asked.

"I am condemned to be a slave to my treasure," the ghost answered. "It was bought with human tears and suffering—and now I am tied to it until someone takes it and sets me free."

The ghost opened up a hole in the floor and pointed. The young man saw the glow of gold, silver, and jewels, gleaming in the faint firelight. "Take it!" Jean Lafitte begged. "Take it all. Only then will my soul be saved."

He reached out to the young man, his fingers dripping blood. His touch was like ice, and the young man shuddered. He plunged out of the house into the storm and ran as far and as fast he could.

Eventually, the young man made his way home. He warned everyone he met about the pirate's treasure, for he was convinced that whoever took the gold and jewels would also inherit the pirate's curse.

This creepy story has been told for centuries—and variations of it are still being told at pajama parties across North America.

A little boy named John lived next door to a little girl named Jane. Jane always wore a shiny yellow ribbon around her neck. "Why do you always wear that ribbon?" John asked her one day.

Jane shrugged. "Ask me again later."

As Jane and John grew older, they spent all their time together. When it was time for their senior prom, they went together. Jane wore a beautiful long dress—and the yellow ribbon around her neck. "Why do you always wear that ribbon?" John asked her.

Jane smiled. "Ask me again later."

John and Jane fell in love and decided to get married. On their wedding day, Jane wore a lacy white dress—and the yellow ribbon around her neck. "Why are you still wearing that ribbon?" John asked.

Jane gave him a kiss. "Ask me again later."

The years went by, and John and Jane had children. They were very happy together, but Jane always wore the yellow rib-

In today's world of print and the media, oral stories still exist, often told by young people around campfires, at sleepovers, or on long rides in the car or school bus. Surprise endings are an important element of these oral narratives.

For instance, almost everyone has heard "The Golden Arm." Suspense builds as the ghost moans again and again, "Whooo stole my golden arm?"

Few people can resist jumping with fear when the storyteller grabs them and shouts, "You took it!"

John finally learned the answer to his question!

bon around her neck. "Why do you always wear that thing?" John asked her often.

Jane would always reply, "Ask me again later."

At last, John and Jane grew old, and one day Jane was too weak to get out of bed. She knew she was dying.

John sat beside the bed, holding her hand. "Darling," he said, "won't you tell me now why you always wear that yellow ribbon?"

"Untie the ribbon," whispered Jane. "You'll see."

So John gently untied the yellow ribbon.

And Jane's head fell off.

Stories of lovers have become part of our folk tradition.

SEVEN

Love Stories
Romance and Its Consequences

The toad husband proves you can't judge a book by its cover—or a husband by his warts.

ROMANTIC LOVE is one of the most common themes in folktales. The lovers inevitably encounter trials and tribulations, but in the end, Cinderella and her prince fall in love and live happily after, as do Sleeping Beauty and her prince, Beauty and the Beast, and countless other folktale lovers. In the real world, many lovers do live happily ever after—more or less—but not all love affairs go smoothly, and many end in betrayal. Since folklore acts as a reflection of the real world where we live, we find both happy and betrayed lovers in the folktales of North America.

You can't always judge by appearances, as this folktale illustrates. Korean Americans tell this story, but a similar tale is told by European Americans as well.

One day a poor man was fishing for his family's supper, but all he caught was a big, ugly toad. The fisherman was so angry and disappointed that he cursed out loud. The toad rolled its round eyes at the fisherman—and then, to the fisherman's amazement, the toad opened its wide mouth and said in a gentle, croaky voice, "Do not be angry, for one day I will bring you good fortune. Take me home and let me live in your house."

So the fisherman brought the toad home with him, and his wife made it a bed in the corner of the kitchen. She fed it worms and scraps of food, and it grew to be as big as a boy. The fisherman and his wife had no children, but they grew to love the toad as if it were their son.

Lovers come in the most unlikely shapes in folktales!

Near to the fisherman lived a wealthy man with three daughters. One day, the toad announced to his foster parents that he had decided he wanted to marry one of the daughters. His parents were horrified, for they knew the wealthy man would be offended at the very idea, but the toad insisted. At last, his foster mother went to the rich man's house and made the request.

The rich man was so furious at the very idea that he had his servants beat the woman. She came home crying and told the toad what had happened.

"I'm very sorry, Mother," he said. "I will see to my marriage myself. The rich man will be sorry he treated you so poorly."

The toad took a lit lantern and tied it to the foot of a hawk. Then he sent the hawk flying

Toads are popular images in folktales for those who appear unlovely and yet in reality are most deserving of love. In another well-known folktale, the girl must kiss the toad in order to break the magic spell that keeps the prince hidden inside his warty skin. The moral of these stories: *True love reveals the hidden princely qualities in even the most unappealing people.*

above the rich man's house, while he himself hid in the shrubs outside the man's window. As the hawk with the lantern flew past the window, the toad said in a loud, solemn voice, "I have been dispatched by the Heavenly King to tell the master of this house that he will be punished for his arrogance and cruelty if he does not repent. Accept the toad's wedding proposal, or you, your brothers, and your children will be destroyed."

The rich man rushed to the window and looked out. He saw a glowing light hovering in the sky above his house. The toad let go of the string, and the hawk soared higher into the sky, the lantern still on its foot, until at last the light disappeared into the clouds. The rich man was convinced that a heavenly messenger had come to him. He made up his mind to give his youngest daughter to the toad in marriage.

First, he apologized humbly to the toad's foster parents, and then they arranged the marriage. The older girls laughed at their younger sister's bridegroom, but the bride only smiled. Some-

Korean Americans are some of the most recent immigrants to come to North America. Most of them did not immigrate until after 1965, but today Korean businesses and shops are plentiful in many North American cities. Many Koreans attend Korean Protestant churches; their faith, their own foods, and their stories help them find an ongoing identity all their own.

how, she was certain she could come to love the toad. The wedding took place the following day.

After the toad and the girl had gone to bed together, the toad told his new wife, "Go fetch a pair of scissors." Startled, the girl obeyed.

"Now cut the skin off my back," the toad requested.

The girl was horrified at the idea, but the toad insisted, and at last she did as he asked. Carefully, she snipped a long slit down the toad's warty back. To her amazement, a handsome young man stepped out of the skin and took her in his arms.

The next morning, however, the young man slipped into his toad skin once more. The girl's sisters made fun of her for having such an ugly husband, and people pointed and stared. But the toad paid no attention. While the men of the household went out hunting, the toad followed them, hopping along as fast as he could. The hunters had no luck, but when no one was looking, the young man once more stepped out of his toad skin.

He waved his hand, and a hundred deer came running to him. Stepping into his toad skin once more, the young man drove the deer back to the rich man's home. Everyone was astonished to see the toad bringing so many deer, and the sisters' sneers disappeared.

They were even more surprised, however, when the young man threw off his toad skin. He waved his hand again, releasing all the deer. With a smile, he turned to his bride and his parents. "Only you three loved me enough to see past my ugly skin." He gathered them up in his arms and rose with them into Heaven.

The Inuit people of northern Canada and Alaska tell this story of love and betrayal. The tale is also a why-things-are-the-way-they-are myth.

Long ago, the people had no seals and walruses to hunt, only reindeer and bears and birds. The sea held no animals.

At this time, a beautiful girl named Sedna lived with her father by the sea. Men from her village and from faraway came to court her, but she refused to marry them all. None of them pleased her. She was far happier with the company of her dog, her friend since childhood.

One day, however, a handsome young stranger paddled his **kayak** across the sea toward Sedna's home. His clothes were rich and beautiful, and he carried an ivory spear. When he reached the shore's edge, he called to Sedna where she stood watching, "Come with me! Where I live there is never hunger. I live in the land of birds, and if you marry me, you will rest on soft skins at night, you will always have meat, and your lamp will always hold oil."

Sedna only shook her head, but the young stranger told her of the rich furs and ivory necklaces she would have if she became his wife. At last, he persuaded her to join him in his kayak. Together they sailed away from her father's home, far out into the sea.

Suddenly, the young man dropped his paddle and raised his hands toward the sky. Terrified, Sedna watched as his arms turned into enormous wings that lifted him up into the air. He was no man at all, but a spirit **loon**. Shivering with fear and cold, she climbed onto the loon's back, and he flew away with her to his home.

The story of Mr. Fox is similar to the tale of Bluebeard, whose wife discovers that her husband has the dead bodies of women hidden in his house.

The hunters and trappers of the far north told stories to pass the long hours.

The Inuit tale of Sedna is a tragic and bitter love story.

There she discovered that the loon-man had lied to her. Her new home was cold and windy; her only food was the fish the loon and the other birds brought to her. Sedna was lonely and afraid. She wished that her dog was with her to keep her company, and she thought often of her father, longing for him to come and take her home.

After a year had passed, she saw her father's boat sailing toward the loon's land. Joyfully, she ran to meet him, splashing through the shallow waves until he could hear her voice. When she begged him to take her home with him, he lifted her into the boat, and they raced across the sea, back to their home.

When the loon-man found that his wife was gone, he took

the shape of a man and leapt into his kayak. He paddled after his father-in-law until he was close enough to shout, "Let me see my wife."

Sedna's father had pushed her to the bottom of the boat with furs over her head to hide her. He shook his head at his son-in-law and kept on paddling.

"Sedna," the loon-man called, "come back to me! No one else could ever love you as I do."

But Sedna did not move from her hiding place. With a cry of pain, the loon-man raised his arms toward the sky. They turned into huge wings, and he rose over his father-in-law's boat, calling the sad, eerie call of the loon. Then he plunged straight down into the water.

The moment the loon-man disappeared beneath the sea, the waves began to leap and lunge. The sea gods were angry that Sedna had betrayed her husband. They tossed her father's boat back and forth, lashing it with towering waves. Her father was so terrified that at last, to save himself, he pushed Sedna into the water.

Gasping, Sedna rose to the surface and grabbed the edge of her father's boat. Her father was nearly insane with terror, and he stabbed at her hands with his knife, driving his daughter away.

An amazing thing happened then: the blood that flowed from Sedna's fingers into the water took the shape of seals. When Sedna again lunged at the boat with her hands, her father once more lashed at her with his knife. By this time, the sea was red with her blood—and from it swam walruses alongside the seals. With the last of her strength, Sedna tried one last time to grab her father's boat, but again he drove her away—and whales grew from her dark blood as it flowed from her torn hands.

Sedna sank to the bottom of the sea, followed by the creatures that had been born from her blood. Her father, sick at heart and exhausted, made his way home, where he found Sedna's dog howling on the shore.

In the dark of the night, Sedna ordered the sea animals born of her blood to bring her father and her dog to her. The animals obeyed her, and brought Sedna's father and dog down into the depths of the sea. There they have lived ever since.

Inuit hunters pray to Sedna, goddess of the sea, who commands all sea creatures. Her heart is still bitter and torn by her husband's lies and her father's betrayal, and so she often refuses

to release her animals so the Inuit can eat. By her whim, hunters find success at sea—or are swept away by the waves. Her hands still hurt her too much for her to comb her long tangled hair, so brave **medicine men** swim down to her watery home and comb her hair for her. If they comb gently enough, she is pleased, and she releases a seal or a walrus for the people to eat.

North America's English settlers brought with them this story of misplaced love:

Lady Mary was very beautiful and had many suitors—but she loved only Mr. Fox, the most handsome of all her lovers. She

Mr. Fox proved to be not only a worthy lover but a serial killer!

promised to marry him, and she looked forward to seeing her new home. For some reason, though, Mr. Fox never brought her or her brothers to see the fine house where he lived.

Curious, Lady Mary decided to take a look at his house one day when she knew Mr. Fox was away on business. After much searching, she found it and walked through the gate. Above the gateway, she saw these words:

BE BOLD, BE BOLD

Strange, she thought as she continued on to the house. Above the doorway, she saw more words.

BE BOLD, BE BOLD, BUT NOT TOO BOLD

Stranger and stranger, she mused. She went inside the house and up the wide stairs, till she came to a door. Above it, she read:

BE BOLD, BE BOLD, BUT NOT TOO BOLD,
LEST YOUR HEART'S BLOOD SHOULD RUN COLD

But Lady Mary was brave as well as beautiful. She opened the door—and then stood still as stone, hardly daring to breathe, for the room was full of women's bodies, all stained with blood, some fresh and some so old that only skeletons dressed in silk were left.

A noise behind her made her jump and turn, and then she hid behind the door, for Mr. Fox was coming up the stairs, dragging the body of a young woman. Just as he came even with Lady Mary, he saw a diamond ring glittering on the dead woman's finger. He tried to pull it off, but when it refused to budge, he drew his sword and cut off the young woman's hand. It jumped in the

Stories about lovers are part of folklore across North America. Have you heard stories about these famous lovers?

Bonnie and Clyde
King Arthur and Guinevere
John and Abigail Adams
Frankie and Johnny
Cinderella and the Prince
Beauty and the Beast
Romeo and Juliet
Barbara Allen and Sweet Willie
Fair Ellen and Lord Thomas

Pieces of these same love stories show up over and over in folktales and folk songs, as well as in popular songs, novels, and movies.

air and landed in Lady Mary's lap. He looked around for it, but he had other matters on his mind. When the door closed behind him, Lady Mary raced as fast as she could out of the house.

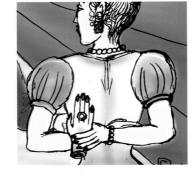

The next day Mr. Fox came to finalize their marriage agreement. "I had a terrible dream last night," Lady Mary told him. She described to him what she had seen in his house.

Mr. Fox only smiled. "It is not so, nor was it so. God forbid that it be so."

"But it is so," Lady Mary cried. "Here's hand and ring I have to show."

She drew the lady's hand out of her pocket and pointed them at Mr. Fox. Before he could say a thing to defend himself, her brothers had surrounded him, with their swords drawn.

Most folktales are full of fanciful and even irrational events; legends, however, are more rooted in the real world.

EIGHT

Historical Legends
Kernels of Truth

Stories of Jesse James have become a part of North America's folk legends.

PROBABLY MOST folktales have at least some small kernel of fact at their center, like a tiny seed that started the whole thing growing, but in most cases it's pretty hard to identify that little piece of fact. (After all, when you look at an oak tree towering over your head, you don't automatically picture the acorn that was the start of all that vegetation.) But in some cases, the facts are recent enough or well known enough, that they're easily recognized. In those cases, it's sometimes hard to separate the folktale from history.

For example, Jesse James was a real person. Historians know quite a bit about Jesse, and you can find his name in almost any book of North American history. But Jesse was also a folk hero, and stories and legends grew up around him. These stories were probably rooted in fact, but as they were told and retold, they got embellished along the way. Something that happened a hundred miles away was moved to the teller's own neighborhood; a daring feat was exaggerated out of proportion; something that happened to the acquaintance of an acquaintance now took place in the life of the teller's own grandfather.

Back in the 1930s, when the Federal Writers Project was collecting folklore from around the United States, a man in Indiana told the following story to one of the collectors. The man claimed that the story was a true one told by his great-grandfather.

JESSE James used to ride through Indiana quite often, in between his rampages when he'd have to lay low for a while. The man was an outlaw of course, but he wasn't so bad as the lawmen

made out. In fact, Jesse was a regular Robin Hood, stealing from the rich so he could give to the poor. And lots of times he was blamed for stealing he didn't do at all.

One night just before dark, a man rode up to a roadside inn [owned by the teller's grandfather]. His big white horse was lathered up, as though it had been ridden hard, but the man seemed calm and quiet. He asked for a room and went to bed.

The next morning, as the family was eating breakfast with their guest, they noticed two pearl-handled pistols sticking out of the man's coat as it hung on the peg by the door. But the man finished his breakfast quietly and went on his way.

About noon, the lawmen came riding up to the inn, looking for Jesse James. He'd been last seen riding a big white horse.

NOTHING much happens in a legend like this, but it's enough to give the teller a sense that he's connected to history—particularly since his own home is built in the same spot as his great-grandfather's inn. People across Indiana have their own family legends to tell about the time Jesse James stayed in their home. They can even point to the bullet holes his gun left in their barns.

Legends like these don't only belong to the more distant past. In the 20th and 21st cen-

This picture is a newspaper drawing of the scene where Jesse James was finally shot and killed.

For centuries, people have been reluctant to let go of their heroes, even in the face of death. Like JFK and Elvis Presley, King Arthur, the long-ago legendary hero, is said to have never really died. According to legend, he too will return when his country needs him most.

turies, people still pass along legends that arise around famous figures of the day. For instance, according to one folk legend, John F. Kennedy is still alive. One teller of this particular legend knew it was true because she had heard it from a friend, who heard it from her cousin, who heard it from his friend, who heard from another friend.

PRESIDENT Kennedy is still alive to this very day. (After all, he'd only be in his 80s by now.) Of course, he's not much more than a vegetable, since he's brain damaged from the bullet he took in his brain. But he's alive.

Seems the doctors were able to save his life after the terrible events in November 1963. Unfortunately, they could do nothing to bring the President out of his coma. Rather than create a national and international uproar, the inner circle of the government decided it would be better if everyone thought Kennedy was dead. That way Johnson could take over, and life would go on.

So they moved Kennedy up to the third floor of the hospital where he was taken after he was shot. There he was kept hidden from the world. Rumors escaped, however, telling of mysterious visits to the hospital's third floor by the CIA and the Secret Service—and once a beautiful dark-haired woman wearing sunglasses.

All hope is not lost, though, for medical research is progressing each and every day. One day, doctors will transplant someone's brain cells into the damaged area of Kennedy's brain. Then he will leave the hos-

Folk legends have also arisen around the events connected to other outlaws, including Al Capone and John Dillinger. One man even claimed that Dillinger was a kindly man who would give pocket money to children; he and his gang were even said to help poor folk clear their land and work their gardens.

One early folklorist, Jacob Grimm, made a distinction between legends based on historical facts and folktales. He wrote:

> The folktale is with good reason distinguished from the legend, though by turns they play into one another. Looser, less fettered than legend, the folktale lacks that local habitation which hampers legend, but makes it more home-like. The folktale flies, the legend walks, knocks at your door; the one can draw freely out of the fullness of poetry, the other has almost the authority of history.

Another folklorist, Wayland Hand, observed that a strong element of belief is what sets the legend apart from other folktales. And folklorist Alan Jabbour notes that time is the main difference between the two forms of stories: the folktale has a mythic, "once-upon-a-time" timeframe outside our normal domain of time, while the legend is set in the historical past.

pital and come back to help his country once more, perhaps in her greatest crisis.

IN some stories, Kennedy was eventually spirited away to the private island of his wife's new husband. Sometimes, people even claim to have caught a glimpse of Kennedy. Similar stories having to do with music idols like Elvis Presley and John Lennon also circulate North America.

Legends like these are a way of giving people a sense of importance and identity. The fame and power of larger-than-life figures seems to rub off a little on the tellers. What's more, in the face of tragedy, violence, and corruption, legends create a world that is full of hope.

Folktales often deal with images of death.

NINE

Ever After

Stories About Death and the World to Come

In some stories, death is a person.

FOLKTALES REFLECT the themes that interest humanity most. Some have to do with courage, some with wonder, some with love—and some have to do with death. Death is the ultimate mystery. Human beings fear the unknown, yet they are fascinated by it as well. And what frightens and fascinates them, inspires them to make stories.

Sometimes folktales picture Death as a land—and sometimes as a person. German Americans tell this story about the inevitability of death.

A poor man had 12 children he could barely feed. When the 13th was born, he ran out into the road, determined to ask the first person he met to be the child's godfather.

The first he met was God himself. "Poor man," God said, "I know how hard your life is. I will hold your child at his christening, and I will care for him all through his life."

"Who are you?" the man asked.

"I am God."

"Then I don't want you to be my child's godfather." The man was suddenly filled with anger and resentment. "You give to the rich and leave the poor hungry!" He turned away from God and went further down the road.

Before long, he met the Devil. "Let me be your child's godfather," the Evil One said. "I will give him gold and all the world's pleasures."

"Who are you?" asked the man.

"I am the Devil."

According to Greek legend, Orpheus traveled to the land of the dead seeking his beloved wife Eurydice. Like the Ojibwa boy, Orpheus had to cross the water that separated him from Eurydice, and like the boy, Orpheus is forced to leave his loved one behind. The Greek view of death, however, was bleak and frightening, while the Native American perspective was far more hopeful. In the Ojibwa story, the memory of a departed loved one—the girl's shadow—is a gift, one that directs a person's life toward goodness.

"I don't want you to be my child's godfather," the man cried. "You are a liar and a cheat." And he went on his way.

Then along came Death, hobbling on withered legs. "Take me as your child's godfather."

"Who are you?" asked the man.

"I am Death, and I make all things equal."

"Then you are the one I want to be my child's godfather, for you treat the rich and the poor the same."

Death replied, "I will make your child rich and famous. You have chosen wisely."

So Death became the child's godfather, and when the boy had grown into a man, Death told him, "I will make you a famous doctor. When you are called to a patient, if I stand by the head, you may tell everyone that the sick person will recover. Give the person this medicine and he will get well. But if I stand by the patient's foot, you must tell everyone that no remedy can cure this person. Never use my medicine against my will."

Soon the young man was the most famous doctor in the land.

People came from all over the world to be treated by him, and he grew very wealthy. One day he was even called to treat the King himself.

When the doctor came to the King's bed, he saw Death standing at the foot of the bed. But the young man did not want the King to die, and he had the bed moved, so that now Death stood at his head. Then he gave the King the medicine Death had given him, and the King recovered.

But Death was furious with the doctor. "You have disobeyed me! Since you are my godson I will forgive you this once, but if you ever do so again, I will take you instead of your patient away with me."

A few years later, the King's only daughter fell ill. The King promised that whoever could make her well, could marry the princess. When the young man came to the girl's sickbed, he saw that she was very beautiful, and he longed to marry her. But there was Death standing at her feet.

The young man was too in love to care. He raised the girl up in his arms and then laid her back on the bed, this time with her feet where her head had been, and then he gave her the medicine. Instantly, her cheeks grew flushed with color, and she sat up and kissed the young man.

But Death stood tall and dark, waiting to speak with the young doctor. "Your life is over now," Death said, and he seized the young man in his cold hands and carried him down into a dark cave.

Thousands and thousands of candles were burning in the darkness, in long, glimmering rows. As the young man stared at them, they seemed to spark and dance, and the young man realized that every instant some candles were going out while others were leaping into flame.

"These are the lights of human lives," Death said. "In most cases, the tall ones belong to children, the medium-sized ones to people in the prime of their lives, and the shorts one to old people."

"Show me the light of my life," the young man said, thinking that it would still be very tall.

To his horror, Death pointed to a small, flickering light that was ready to go out. "There, that is yours."

"Dear godfather," the young man begged, "light a new candle for me. I want to marry the princess and be happy with her. I want to be king one day and the father of many children."

Death shook his head. "I cannot light you a new candle, for one must go out before a new one is lit. You should have obeyed me."

Then he leaned forward and blew out the young man's candle.

Not all death stories are **pessimistic** *and gloomy. The Ojibwa people tell this story of love and hope that are strong enough to endure beyond the barrier of death.*

Once two orphan children lived together in the forest, a boy and a girl who depended on each other for companionship and care. They loved each other dearly and were happy together, until a bitter winter froze the land where they lived. Unable to find enough food, they grew thin and gaunt, and eventually the sister died.

Heartbroken and lonely, the boy resolved to follow his sister into the land of the dead. He would either live there with her—

In many stories, a wide river separates the land of the living from the land of death.

The Ojibwa (also known as the Chippewa) are Native Americans who live in Canada and the United States, from Lake Huron west into Saskatchewan and North Dakota. They speak a version of the Algonquian language.

or bring her back with him to the land of the living. So he set off on his journey, traveling always westward.

At last he reached the Great Water that separates the living from the dead. A wrinkled old man stopped him and said, "What are you doing here?"

When the boy explained that he was seeking his sister, the old man shook his head. "You have undertaken a difficult journey, but I will help you. Your sister passed this way several months ago, and by now she has entered the Land of Shadows, where disease and pain are unknown. No one wearies or grows old there—but to get to her, you must cross this sea, and the way is treacherous."

He showed the boy a beautiful canoe carved from white stone. "This will take you across the sea." Then he handed the boy a pipe and a pouch of tobacco. "Keep this, for you will have need of it."

Night had fallen, but the boy would not wait to begin his voyage across the water. He said good-bye to the old man, and set off, paddling through the steep waves that threatened to overwhelm his canoe. All around him, he caught glimpses of other white canoes, just like his, but they all seemed to be empty. He called across the water, hoping someone would answer, but all he heard was the moaning of the wind.

After several days, the sea grew calm, and the boy saw a sweet, green land ahead of him. He beached the canoe and set out to find his sister.

As he walked, he nearly tripped over something that lay across his path. It was a skeleton, bleached white in the sun. To his amazement, with a click and a clack of bony ribs and legs, the skeleton sat up. "Why are you here?" the skeleton asked the boy. "You don't belong here."

When the boy had told the skeleton his story, the skeleton said, "I may be able to help you find your sister. But first, let me smoke your pipe."

As the skeleton puffed on the pipe, wisps of smoke drifted out between his ribs; when the smoke floated upward, it turned into doves. The skeleton flapped a bony hand at the white birds. "Follow them. They will lead you to your sister."

The boy followed the white doves as they fluttered through a pine forest and finally led him into a fragrant garden. All around him he could hear the sound of human voices, but he could see no one. He realized, however, that the shadows that flickered across the grass were the shape of human beings.

Then his heart leapt with joy, for he recognized his sister's voice. He stared hard at the shadows, until he was certain he knew which one was hers. "Come home with me!" he cried. "I am so sad and lonely without you."

His sister's voice answered him sadly. "I cannot go back with you now, for I have eaten of the fruit of this land. Had you come sooner, I would have gone with you, but now it is impossible."

"Then I will stay here with you!"

But his sister explained to him that he had much still to do in life. He would be a great chief, a leader of peace and mercy for his people. Sorrowfully, the boy accepted that he must return to the land of the living and do his work in life.

"Take my shadow with you," the girl told him before he left. "It is my gift to you. When it is with you, no evil will come to you, for it can be present only in light—and where there is light, no evil can lurk. Be on your guard, Brother, for if you see the shadow disappear, you will know that darkness has come upon you."

The boy took his sister's shadow and bid her farewell. Then

Immigrants from the British Isles may have brought this story of death with them to the New World:

An old woman lay for a long while on the point of death, but to the surprise of all, she continued to hang on to life. At last her relatives and friends discussed the problem.

"Well," said one, "she isn't gone yet, nor will she be any time soon by the looks of things."

"Poor, dear soul," said another, "she's going slow, sure enough."

"I tell you want," chimed in an older woman, "I think she's lying the wrong ways around. Her body can't slip through the door into death because it's lying crosswise like."

So with much effort, together the woman's friends and family lifted her old-fashioned bedstead and managed to turn it around in the tiny room.

Some hours later when the doctor called to see his patient, the woman's daughter greeted him at the door. "She's gone, doctor. We just shifted her bed round, and she went off like a lamb!"

he sailed back across the sea to the Land of the Living. He lived to be an old man, a great leader of his people. When he died, he vanished like snow, taking his sister's shadow with him. He had gone to be with her in the Land of Shadows, where they are once more happy together.

Stories lean on stories. . . .
It is the story of the world.
And when that story is finally at an end,
so too ends the world.

—Jane Yolen

Further Reading

Ancelet, Barry Jean. *Cajun and Creole Folktales*. New York: Garland, 1994.

Bierhorst, John. *Latin American Folktales*. New York: Pantheon, 2002.

Fowke, Edith. *Legends Told in Canada*. Toronto: Royal Canadian Museum, 1994.

Leeming, David and Jake Page. *Myths, Legends, and Folktales of America*. New York: Oxford, 1999.

Stewart, R. J. *Celtic Myths, Celtic Legends*. New York: Sterling, 1997.

Yolen, Jane. *Favorite Folktales from Around the World*. New York: Pantheon, 1986.

For More Information

Folktales from China
www.pitt.edu/~dash/china.html

Folktales from Japan
www.pitt.edu

Folktales, Tall Tales, and Legends
www.aaronshep.com/stories/

Myths, Folktales, and Fairy Tales
teacher.scholastic.com

Russian Folktales
www.geocities.com/Athens/Agora/5873/

Glossary

Bayou A swampy area in Louisiana.

Cajuns The French settlers from Acadia in Canada who migrated south to Louisiana.

Cutlass A short, curved sword.

Genealogies Records of a person or family's descent from ancestors.

Ingenuity Cleverness, inventiveness.

Kayak A canoe made of skins with only a small opening in the center.

Loon A large water bird.

Medicine men Wise men or shamans.

Pessimistic Always expecting the worst to happen.

Venerated Respected and revered.

Index

Biographies

Ellyn Sanna has authored more than 50 books, including adult nonfiction, novels, young adult biographies, and gift books. She also works as a freelance editor and helps care for three children, a cat, a rabbit, a one-eyed hamster, two turtles, and a hermit crab.

Dr. Alan Jabbour is a folklorist who served as the founding director of the American Folklife Center at the Library of Congress from 1976 to 1999. Previously, he began the grant-giving program in folk arts at the National Endowment for the Arts (1974–1976). A native of Jacksonville, Florida, he was trained at the University of Miami (B.A.) and Duke University (M.A., Ph.D.). A violinist from childhood on, he documented oldtime fiddling in the Upper South in the 1960s and 1970s. A specialist in instrumental folk music, he is known as a fiddler himself, an art he acquired directly from elderly fiddlers in North Carolina, Virginia, and West Virginia. He has taught folklore and folk music at UCLA and the University of Maryland and has published widely in the field.